BIKERS STEAL MY HUSBAND

Straight to Gay MMM

Michael Levi

CONTENTS

Title Page

Copyright

Chapter 1 — 1

Chapter 2 — 6

Chapter 3 — 11

Chapter 4 — 16

Chapter 5 — 21

Chapter 6 — 26

Epilogue — 30

Sneak Peek: Caught Looking by the Quarterback — 35

Bicurious Series and More — 39

About the Author — 41

CHAPTER 1

I peered out the window of the living room, finding something that made my heart jump. It was my wife and she was with *them*. One of the bikers had his arm wrapped around her lower back, pulling her slightly closer to him. The audacity of that guy... I should be furious with Sandra, but the fact was that I wasn't. I should also be livid at the biker, but I also wasn't.

Even though my heart was tight, I was paralyzed where I was. I had no idea what to do, especially because my wife had always been loyal to me this whole time, and I had always been loyal to her.

She was the most precious person in the world to me, and that would never change. Not even those rough bikers could dent that part of my life, and it was almost like a promise I was making to myself.

I clenched my hand. It wasn't like I was going to stay hidden in the living room, not doing anything while they were drooling over my wife and showing no shame while their fingers explored her body.

Not to mention that she walked out wearing little more than I was comfortable with, and it showed more of her skin than it should.

Especially her chest cleavage showing her ample, heavy, and dare I say succulent milkers. Oh, I just missed them so much. I was aware that our relationship had grown stale recently, but she still never cheated on me, and I planned on keeping things that way.

And yet, something about those bikers was making me

develop an alien feeling. My cock was getting harder in my pants and it was something that never happened before, especially when I was watching any man from afar.

Those bikers didn't have anything special, other than looking like such massive, heavy beasts, their muscles almost bursting out of their clothes and threatening to make me look smaller than I was, something that was unthinkable not too long ago.

And even though I was fighting against it, my hand moved down and cupped my crotch. If my wife was seeing me doing this now, she would probably find it funny. The reason was that she always thought I was beyond doing something like this, and she was right.

I shouldn't even be admiring those bikers, and it didn't matter how tough-looking and how perfect their bodies were. None of those things mattered, and yet I was still feeling so hot right now.

So much so that I could feel a layer of sweat covering my forehead, and I had no idea what to do about that.

I sighed, shaking my head. Even though it didn't make any sense, I wanted to jerk off while thinking about those massive, rough bikers dominating my wife in all the ways they could. The things that they would be able to do while I watched... Just thinking about them was arousing me. Those bikers weren't doing anything special, but they were already reminding me how puny I was in comparison to them.

My body was much smaller, even though I worked out. I hit the gym a couple of times every week and I thought I was making some progress, only to realize that it was pointless, especially in comparison to those bikers.

They were so much bigger and heavier than me that I was pretty sure just one punch from them would knock me out cold, and it was something I didn't say often about myself.

Even though my hand was shaking, especially because I didn't want to confront the bikers from The Prowlers MC, there was no point in denying the inevitable.

I stepped outside my home and the first thing that came into my mind was that I was hoping Sandra was going to notice me and then turn around and come back inside, almost like nothing happened.

But I glanced up, my eyes moving slowly, and I realized that she wasn't. She didn't notice me and the dirty smile on her face was telling.

She was enjoying all the attention she was getting from the bikers, their bodies far too close to hers, making her look even smaller than she was. If I thought that I was small in comparison to them, it was even more so with her. She was like an insignificant blip on their radar, and that realization was making my cock stir in my pants.

I would enjoy watching those bikers devouring my wife. They would destroy her holes so intensely that she would almost blackout. Maybe I was a little more loyal to her than I should be, especially because no man in his right mind should be thinking that way about his wife. I wasn't a cuck and I wasn't going to become one. I couldn't even imagine what my family would think if they found out that I handed my wife over to two dirty bikers. I was just not going to let that happen, no matter the cost.

I was approaching them when they turned their eyes to me, freezing me where I was. Even though I froze, my eyes still studied them from their feet to their forehead, and I couldn't describe what I was feeling. It was something alien, making my rod grow bigger in my pants.

Maybe I should be worried about the boner that was soon going to show up, even though it was going to be so small and insignificant that the bikers weren't even going to glance down at it, not to mention that my wife was much more appetizing in terms of looks, too.

I liked to think that I was good-looking, but for macho-men like those cowboys… They couldn't care less about me.

Even though it took everything I had, I still took another step toward them and I wasn't surprised when they burst out laughing.

"You her hubby, little guy?" The biker on the right asked, seated on his motorcycle. The motorcycle was as massive and as heavy as he was, and also just as imposing. Just looking at it, finding all the details made of silver and chrome, I couldn't even imagine myself sitting on it. I knew it would almost behave like a horse, kicking me off of it.

I just couldn't hide the lust that was in my eyes. I was already thinking about doing it, even though I shouldn't. I wondered what it would be like if these bikers finally lowered their pants and showed me what they were packing. And it wasn't like they were hiding their bulges, either. I had no idea if it was their form-fitting jeans or something else, but I could see their bulges clearly and they were enormous, and also hefty.

Saliva was building up in my mouth and I had no idea what to do. I was still trying to do everything in my power so that they didn't notice my crush on them, but it was pointless. They were perceptive bikers, I could tell.

I nodded. There was no point in not answering his question, and I knew that if I didn't do it, he would be pissed. And if he was pissed, things would get out of control in a heartbeat.

"I'm Gears and this is Forger," the biker on the right side, and I noticed that they were almost like twins. They were eerily similar, something I thought I would never witness in my life. They were so similar that it made them hotter than they were.

Their head shape, their lips, their noses, and those rippling and flexing muscles... Everything about them reminded me of who I could be if things were different, if I had more self-esteem.

I didn't say anything, my cheeks flushing red. I was so jealous of them that I couldn't even come up with the right words. They said their names and they were expecting me to tell them my name, but I was just no good with introductions, not to mention that their dominant presence was making me feel even more insignificant.

It was like I was in college and about to give a presentation to my class, something I hadn't thought about in a very long time.

Eventually, I managed to muster up enough strength. "I'm Casen, her husband." And saying that, she chuckled. I knew she was going to find the way I said my name funny, but it still hurt me, especially seeing the way that she was in their arms, between their motorcycles, their low rumbling reverberating in the air around us. It was like time froze around us and I could do nothing about it.

I felt he was so entangled with what was going on that I just had to accept my fate. I was still trying hard to say to myself that I wasn't gay, but that was growing more confusing and difficult as time passed.

I guessed there was no more point in fighting back against it.

CHAPTER 2

"You like feeling my hand moving like this over your shoulder, don't you?" The biker asked my wife, and I saw her melting in his arms, throwing her arms around his neck and pressing her boobs to his wide, sweaty chest. Even though she was quite busty, she still looked so small, especially against his much more advantageous frame.

I could almost see my old self shouting in my face, asking what the hell was even going on with me right now. I should be stronger than this, I should be reclaiming my wife, but I was actually thinking about doing something else.

Even though the question was most likely directed to my wife, I still felt like it was for me. I supposed it was for that reason that I answered, "I don't like it. She's my wife, and I'm always going to do everything I can to protect her."

She burst out laughing again, grinning from ear to ear. I could see the way she was rubbing her body against the biker's and it was pissing me off as much as it was turning me on. I was already beginning to wonder what the biker looked like, especially without his shirt and leather jacket on. His ripped, well-toned body would put mine to shame, and it wouldn't even be the beginning of it.

"I like the way he moves his hand over me, and even though you're trying to hide it well, I know you think the same way," she said, her tone showing that she was joking about it, even though it told the truth.

"Sandra, what happened between us? I woke up today and

found you like this, entangled between these bikers and hitting on them. It's pathetic and it's making me feel useless. I thought you were loyal to me."

"I *am* loyal, but I still crave something different sometimes, and today it's about that," she replied, putting her head on Forger's chest and then pointing down with her finger to my crotch. I knew what she was going to say before she said it. "Honey, I know you're trying to hide it, but it's okay. I know that these bikers are making you feel something different, something alien, but it's nothing like that. I knew you were always bi."

And that accusation, even though it was the truth, wasn't something I was going to let slide. I was going to do something about it, and it was going to be now, even though my pathetic and small frame didn't hold a candle to those bikers.

Their presence was enough to remind me of that, and the tattoos on their bodies... they only made me feel even more insignificant than I was.

I licked my lips and I knew that it was a mistake. So much so that I wasn't surprised when Forger winked at me, his bulge growing bigger. And I supposed I shouldn't be surprised when I saw my wife's hand moving around it, cupping it, applying pressure on it even through his jean pants. She was enjoying every minute of this, and it was telling. It wasn't that she was loyal to me or anything of the sort. She was looking for someone that could dominate her, bend her over on our bed, and I wasn't that person. Not anymore. She was probably even wondering why she married me.

I could feel my knees wobbling and my legs trembling. It was something that hadn't happened in a very long time and I still had no idea how to deal with it.

"This is all entertaining and all, but I'm already getting bored," Gears said, turning off his bike and then stepping toward me. If I thought before that I was small, now it was even more evident.

He was growing bigger in my vision, and it was like he was turning into this huge, uncontrollable beast that was going to bend me to his will.

And he kept on approaching me and I didn't know what to do to make him stop. It was like he knew everything. He knew I had a huge crush on him and his buddy, and that there was nothing I could do against it, other than accept it. And I was.

I could see the way his muscles were almost ripping his shirt and leather jacket off, his jeans curving around his legs, his boner in his pants, and pretty much everything else that defined his body, which was God-like.

"Let's go inside," he proposed and I knew there was no point in going up against that. If I said I didn't want to go back inside my own house, he would laugh at me, and even though that would turn me on more than I already was, I didn't want to see what the consequences of that would be.

He already thought I was someone he could control easily, and that would only make him believe that more strongly.

I just nodded and when my wife was by my side, I tried to grab her hand, but she swatted it. I noticed she had her arm linked with Gears, and he was marching with confidence toward my house.

He was the one that opened the door, and I followed them from behind. In no moment at all, I was back inside my living room, and it felt alien. It also felt tighter and smaller than normal, and that was most likely thanks to the massive and tall bikers that now also occupied it.

"This is actually a pretty cozy place," Gears commented, his arm wrapped around my wife's backside, almost like he was telling me that she was his property and that there was nothing I could do against that.

Nothing that would change anything, of course. I was so certain of that I was already admitting that I was a beta man about to be cucked hard.

"Thanks," I said like the good little pet that I was turning out to be. These bikers were in my living room and I was letting them do whatever they wanted, even though, right now, that wasn't much.

They were just standing there, turning their heads around slightly, checking out my place. Maybe they were thinking they were going to rob the place clean, but even if that was the case, I wouldn't be too opposed to it, and the reason was that I truly was their pet.

"Come here, little Princess. I know your husband can't please you anymore, and we need to do something about that," Gears proposed, plopping down on my couch, on the part of it where I usually sat. It was like he was stealing my place as this house's main man and there was nothing I could do about it. I was letting it happen, and I was enjoying it as well.

He looked up after sitting down on the couch, finding my trembling eyes. "Are you going to do something about this? Are you going to try and stand in my way?" He asked, confronting me. I knew what answer he was looking for and I didn't like it. And yet, there was nothing I could do about it.

Even though they didn't need them, they were armed. I could see the metallic glints of the barrels of their guns at their waistlines. Even if I managed to overwhelm them, they could just shoot me quickly, and I wouldn't even know what was happening until it was too late.

"I'm not going to do anything because I'm a cuck," I confessed and it was the truth. I was beginning to accept my position as their submissive pet, and I was loving it. It was making my heart warm, which was something I thought would never happen.

He smiled devilishly. "That you are, and now, come here. I think there's something you want to do and that your wife will enjoy watching," he demanded, widening his smile.

Even though he didn't say what it was, my suspicion was too strong not to have a good guess about it. I stepped toward him taking short, controlled steps. My arms were almost glued to my body, and I could feel my asshole so tight. I knew that they were thinking about breaching it, even though it wasn't going to happen now.

When I was right in front of him, he made a quick movement with his finger, suggesting that I should go down to my knees. And that I did, falling to my knees before him. Gears had his legs spread out wide and my wife was sitting on his right leg.

It was thick enough for her ample ass, something that I never thought possible. In fact, the longer this was going on, the more I was feeling like these bikers were growing bigger.

They were almost inhuman.

CHAPTER 3

"Lower my pants and suck me off," Gears said and I knew it wasn't a request, but an order. He wanted me to follow all of his rules, and I was going to do it. My throat was dry, I felt like the air around me was getting hotter and thinner, but I was still going to do it, and it wasn't because it was my calling or anything of the sort, but because I was overly curious. I wanted to see his dick and given that he was willing and this wasn't a dream, there was no point in hiding the truth.

My hands were shaking, but it was okay. My wife positioned herself on top of the arm of the couch and then Gears lifted up his butt, letting me lower his pants.

And I did that, and the moment that his bulge, with only his underwear covering it, was in my eyesight, it was like stars were exploding in my mind.

My throat was even drier than before, and I felt completely lost. I knew what he wanted me to do, but I had no idea how to go about it. I felt so humiliated, especially because my wife was watching this unravel before her eyes and wasn't doing anything about it. She was checking out her nails, most likely waiting until this was over and she could have her fun with her massive, brawny biker.

"Hurry up already, Casen. You are annoying me. You shouldn't be taking your time like this," she grumbled and even though she had a point, it wasn't like it was going to make me more strong-willed all of a sudden. My prick was stiff and leaking pre-cum, and there was nothing I could do about that.

I was finally admitting to myself that I was gay and there was no coming back after this. I could already imagine these bikers coming back here many more times in the future, seeking more of this. And that realization was making me so much harder.

And then my eyes noticed the stain of his pre-cum in his underwear. It was dirty, but even though it was a little nasty, it was also extremely lust-inducing.

If I thought before that I was sweating, now I was even more so. It was like I just finished running a marathon, and it was something that didn't happen often. My job was working at a museum as a curator, so I knew what I was talking about.

"Forger, give me one," he asked, lifting his hand and opening it. Forger gave him a cigarette and then he lit it up with his lighter. He was going to smoke inside my home, and I didn't consider opposing that.

If I did anything that could piss them off, who knew what would happen, and I wasn't willing to take the risk.

He put the butt of the cigarette between his lips, puffing out a large cloud of smoke through his nostrils a moment later. I felt the smoke swirling into my lungs and instead of holding my breath, I welcomed all the nicotine, which was one other thing I thought I would never do in my life. There was something erotic about the smoke, and perhaps that was knowing it was in his lugs before I smelled it. Like it was a part of him I could feel and not touch, but which still reaffirmed his dominance over me.

"I'm also already getting a little annoyed by how slowly this is happening," Forger grumbled, leaning against the doorway and then crossing his arms over his wide chest. I knew what he was talking about, and that made me gulp. I swallowed down the lump that was in my throat, which was something I should have done before.

And he was in the right. I was doing this slowly because I was afraid. I was afraid of what I was going to see. When his cock was finally out of its 'cage', I would feel even smaller than I was already feeling.

And yet, my throat was so dry. I could not stop wondering

about what his manhood looked like, and I was pretty sure he was enjoying that. I looked up, finding Gears' eyes, and I could almost feel the disdain in his eyes. He was enjoying every minute of this, and it was telling.

"Come on, what are you waiting for?" He asked and I inched my hand closer to the band of his dirty pair of briefs.

I could feel the heat of his body pulsing out of it, and it was making the air around me hotter than it should be. It wasn't even hot outside, or not yet, anyway, I remembered. It was going to be the spring season soon, but it wasn't at the moment.

I snuck my fingers under his underwear and then finally pulled it down. I noticed Sandra shifting slightly where she was seated, most likely finding this as enticing as I was. "Oh, I definitely gotta see this," she murmured and that confirmed my suspicion. Everything she was doing was only serving to further humiliate me and I didn't know what to do about it.

There was nothing that could be done, I reminded myself.

I finished lowering his underwear and then he let his ass drop back onto the couch, grinning devilishly. Even though he was a biker, his teeth weren't too bad. They weren't like what one would see in a toothpaste commercial, but they were straight and not at all too dirty – they were whiter than they should be, that was for sure.

But I was just rambling. There was no point in paying so much attention to his teeth, especially because he probably thought little of them. I didn't imagine that he brushed his teeth often. Not like I did, anyway.

And then, I could finally see his prick out of its cage, and it was bigger than I thought. Much, much more so. It was already hard and pointing up, slightly curved to the left. It was riddled with veins, and there was even a big, thick one that snaked up from the base almost all the way to the top, and it was mean and I could see it pumping his blood. It took a lot of blood to keep his dick up, and I could see that.

And his balls... They hung low. He didn't shave before this, and I could see the hair on his ballsack. It was a shame, really. I wished he had shaved before now so that I could see his ballsack even more perfectly than now, but I shouldn't complain about something so insignificant.

It was enough that I was seeing his manhood this way, that I was this close to it, and it took my breath away. For a moment, I thought I couldn't even breathe, but then I realized that I was just holding my breath. I let it out and then the bigger, more imposing man in front of me noticed it. He chuckled.

"Stop taking your time with this. I know you are chicken, but c'mon. Your wife is watching you and she wants to find out if you are a good cocksucker."

I glanced to the right, finding Sandra still perched on the arm of the couch, her arm wrapped over his shoulders and kissing and worshiping the side of his face, her tongue sliding over his skin, tasting him. She was doing that without showing any shame, and I knew she wasn't feeling any of it. When it came down to it, she was a slut. I supposed it was one of the reasons why I fell in love with her.

And it was humiliating me more than I already was being.

"Do I have your permission to touch your mighty cock, sir?" I feebly asked, looking up and finding his eyes. He was staring at me like he didn't care about me, and I knew that was the case. He was doing this just because it made him feel more powerful, as he should be.

He was much more dominant than I was, and he was claiming his rightful place as my wife's lover. And I wasn't doing anything about that because I could see myself becoming his pet for the rest of my life.

He nodded once and slowly, giving me the permission I was looking for. I moved my hand closer to his dick, wrapped my fingers around it, and I noticed that I couldn't make my thumb reach my other fingers. That was how thick he was, and it was much more than I thought humanly possible.

It was like his dick was trembling and pulsing even though I wasn't even doing anything special. I had my hand wrapped around his dick and I was starting to stroke it, and I could also see the pre-come seeping out through the slit.

CHAPTER 4

His pre-come was coating my hand and making my stroking of his dick better and easier. And the best thing about that? It was that I was loving it. I wasn't stopping this, and I shouldn't, anyway. I was finally where I should be and doing the thing I should always have started doing.

I could feel his prick pulsing even harder, more strongly, and then I noticed his balls shifting.

Forger, after having smoked his cigarette, came closer to us. I heard him unzipping his pants and then them falling down onto the floor. He was standing behind me, and I could feel his hand already around his rod.

Even though I wasn't peeking over my shoulder, I knew he had a plan for me, and that there was nothing I could do about it. I could feel shivers running down my spine, coming to that conclusion.

I knew that pleasing one biker was tough, but pleasing two of them at the same time? I had no idea if it was even possible. Was it? I had to know. And it was for that reason that I turned my head to the right, finding his gargantuan prick pointed at me, and it was raging and mean.

"Give it a little kiss," he ordered and I knew I had to do it. I was once a proud husband, thinking about establishing a family with my wife, but know that was all in the past. I was going to be their bitch for the rest of my life, and it showed. It showed in my face and my body language.

My hand was trembling, but I was still stroking Gears'

oversized prick. He was loving that too, tilting his head backward while my wife was still all over him. I was supposed to feel envy, but I couldn't.

If anything, the fact that she was kissing the side of his face and neck, and also massaging his shoulders passionately was turning me on much more than I already was. And the worst thing about that was knowing that no one in here was even going to give me a handjob.

"What are you waiting for, prick?" Gears grumbled without reopening his eyes. He was enjoying every second of this and the only thing that he wanted was that I made him come, which was something I was planning on doing soon. "Hurry up."

I obeyed Forger's order, lowering my head and then kissing the head of his prick. When I felt my tongue and lips touching the tip of it, shivers ran down my spine again. It was so obvious that he was much manlier than me and that his prick was just too big.

"Fuck, that was so good," Forger murmured and then he put his hand on my head, turning it to the left. I was again facing Gears' prick and, this whole time, I didn't stop grabbing it. His dick was still in my hand, and I restarted moving my hand up and down along it, though slowly. I was taking my time, savoring every second of this moment.

The pre-come seeping through the slit was thick, clear, and it kept on coating my fingers and lessening the friction. I was beginning to gain confidence, which was the reason why I started to pick up the pace. It was about time I started to do that.

In the meantime, I had seemingly forgotten about my life. Her hand was still sliding over his chest, brushing his chest hair, and I just noticed how thick it was. He probably never shaved it, which was the opposite of me. I had some chest hair, but it was insignificant. It wasn't as thick and it certainly didn't look as good.

I wished I was the one cherishing his chest hair, but I couldn't.

I had something much more thrilling to deal with and that was his oversized, thick, and heavy penis. It was like it was forcing me to do what I was doing, but it wasn't. I was doing this out of my own volition.

I took a deep breath in, increasing the pace with which my hand was shooting up and down along his dick. When I felt that he was going to come – and I noticed he was indeed going to do that, thanks to his balls tensing up and then his penis throbbing slightly - I decided to do the unthinkable.

I sunk my head, wrapping my lips around his dickhead. It was thick, almost as wide as my mouth, and slightly salty, which was perfect for me. It was exactly the way I was hoping it was.

I was swirling my tongue around his prick, and it was the most delicious thing I tasted in a while. I didn't even know what I was doing, my inexperience showing. And yet, the fact that Gears was moaning was all the incentive I needed right now. That and also the fact that I wrapped my hand around Forger's throbbing slab of meat, and it was just as good.

"Keep it up. You are doing it well," she said and of course it was none other than my wife.

It was a good thing that she was giving me pointers, even though I knew that they were going to be sparse.

"Thanks," I tried to say after stopping for a little bit, trying to make sure that I didn't stop for longer than needed. Since my wife was helping me with giving Gears a blowjob, there was no point in not saying at least thanks to her.

She chuckled. She never thought that I was going to be sucking off the prick of a man, but here I was doing that. And in the meantime, while I was still on my knees on the floor, I wasted no effort before wrapping my fingers around the other biker's dick, who was right behind me.

He was also moaning slightly and I could feel his hand trying to grab the hair of my head, even though doing that was a little difficult right now. My head kept on shooting up and down, giving the man that was sitting on the couch everything he was looking for.

And even that wasn't enough. I was sucking off Gears, but also was giving Forger a handjob that he would never forget. I didn't know who was bigger, but it wasn't like that mattered anyway.

I could feel my hand moving up and down, the speed of it

nothing short of fascinating, and his pre-come coating my fingers and doing a lot more than that. It was easy to give him a handjob and it showed.

My wife pulled out her phone and started to record me. I should feel that it was even more humiliating than this, but I wasn't. It was the right call. She should show everyone just how submissive I was and that I was probably also looking for other partners. I couldn't help but wonder if it would be possible to bring all the other bikers here, making me worship their cocks like it was the last thing I would do with my life.

And giving the man sitting on the couch this blowjob and the other behind me his handjob was more taxing than I thought. My breathing was becoming more ragged, my sweat was covering my entire body, and I could feel I was losing energy. My pace was slowing down, but it started to happen at around the right time.

They started to throb and convulse in my hand and in my mouth, and I knew that they were going to come. When they were cumming, I would swallow every drop of their milk, and it would be the most delicious thing I ever tasted, even more than their pre-cum.

At this point, they were laughing. They didn't have to do much to submit me to their wishes, and it was everything they thought it was going to be.

"You are so funny. I don't know who you thought you were before this, but now you are our bitch," Gears said, but the words barely reached my ears. The reason was that I was so focused on swirling my tongue around his prick and feeling the mushroom shape of his dickhead that I couldn't focus on anything else.

And it was marvelous. It was pressing every right button in me, and it turned me on so much that I couldn't hold it back much longer.

When my climax came, it washed over me. It destroyed me whole, making me convulse, and even his prick slipped out of my mouth, which was something he wasn't pleased with. I knew I was going to get punished for that, but I still didn't care. I loved the direction this was taking, and it was like it was burning my body.

He stood up slowly but suddenly, his eyes glaring at me. "What you just did was unforgivable."

CHAPTER 5

And I stood where I was, looking at the beast of a man in front of me like I didn't know what was happening. I looked so stupid that it was funny, thus I wasn't surprised when they both chuckled at me. Even my wife did that, and it was telling. She was still doing her nails almost like what was happening here was mundane to her.

"I know, but I didn't mean it. I was just having so much fun that when I orgasmed, I felt like my body was being consumed," I tried telling Gears, but I was pretty sure that he wasn't even going to listen to it. In the meantime, I just couldn't stop ogling his massive dick dangling between his legs, and it was still hard.

I could see how wet and slick it looked, and the only thing I wanted right now was to put it back between my lips. Nevertheless, I had no idea if he was even thinking about doing that. His punishment could involve him not letting me touch his manhood ever again, something that hurt me just thinking about it.

Now that I found out how good gay sex was, I didn't want anything else. Imagining myself plunging deep into my wife's pussy? I couldn't even picture myself doing that, not ever again, even though I knew she was tight and was waiting until the guys were done with me. When they were, they were going to be all over her, and I knew I wasn't even going to try stopping them.

"You're pathetic," Forger growled and I noticed my hand was still around his prick, stroking him. He was colossal and every stroke that I gave him reminded me of that, and he was also so warm I just didn't want to move my hand anywhere, something I knew he was already used to.

"I know I am, but I plan on making up for that," I replied meekly and it was the only thing I could do right now. I was under their mercy and they were aware of that. So much so that I knew what they were going to say next before they even revealed it.

"Since you're so pathetic, there's something we need to do about it," Forger said, stepping away from me even though I didn't want him to do that. I thought he was going to be more mindful of my needs, but of course he wasn't even going to think about them.

When it came down to him, his life was only about him and no one else. It was for that reason that he stepped away from me without even looking at me, something that made me feel even more humiliated than I did.

He went outside even though he didn't have his pants on and then came back holding something in his hands. For a moment, my eyes couldn't make out what it was, but then everything clicked.

It was a butt plug, and a big one. I had never seen anything so big and it even had a tail, like that of a cat. They were going to insert the butt plug inside my ass, it was going to stretch my rectum, and that could only mean one thing.

It meant that they were going to breach my asshole, and it could happen at any time. It could even happen today, which was something I was looking forward to. I couldn't help but wonder how I would feel when they were pounding in and out of my ass, eating it raw. I knew I wouldn't be able to sit for days, but I was still welcoming it.

"You ready for this, pussy little man?" He asked, smirking. Of course he was going to be smirking, showing how overconfident he was. It wasn't just about the dick dangling between his legs, his balls that hung too low, and that his scrotum wasn't shaved. It was much more than that. He knew he was always on top, no matter what happened.

I nodded. I knew it was the only thing I could do, and I remembered I was still on my knees on the floor. The right position was to also be with my hands supporting my weight, something I did right away.

They both chuckled, including my wife. In the meantime, Sandra had gone to the kitchen, where she appeared to be whipping up something. I didn't know what it was, but it smelled good. It smelled like something I wanted to eat, which was more than she made for me in the entire time that we were together.

Now that I was thinking about it, was there ever a time when she showed me she was really in love with me? Or was she waiting for these bikers to come here this whole time? I didn't know, but the question hung in the air and I couldn't come up with an answer. I supposed there was none.

He walked until he was behind me and then he squatted, his hands groping my ass. I expected it, but I still arched my back in response. His hands were so warm I couldn't wait until they were all over me, searching every part of me.

I knew he was thinking the same thing, which was for that reason I welcomed everything that was happening here. Even though they were ruthless and were only going to punish me even more than they already were, I was still getting more love from this than I did before in my life.

His fingers slipped between the crack of my ass, looking for my butthole. They found it in little less than a second, and then his fingers were touching and scratching against it, feeling all the ridges and small depressions. He was doing that slowly, obviously taking his time.

He was enjoying every part of my orifice, and in turn, I was in love with that. I was feeling so much more pleasure than when I was sucking off his mate's big dick, and it was evident. They didn't need to stop and study what was going on with me.

"Holy shit, you are a shameless slut," Gears murmured and then I felt something big and cold moving inside my anus, stretching it wide. I knew that it was the buttplug, and I was welcoming it. Every part of it was stretching me so wide that I knew that my rectum would never be the same.

I was sweating and was definitely a little nervous, but it was still the most authentic experience I ever had in my life.

"I'm a slut and I am so for you," I murmured, more to me than to them. They didn't say anything, but they didn't have to. The dirty smirks on their faces told me everything I needed to know, and my body was responding to that.

"When I'm done with you, you will never be the same again," he murmured when his head was close to mine and I could feel the heat radiating out of his body. If I had ever thought that someone could be manlier than he was, then I was confused about it. So much so that I was already making a mental note about that.

His hands groped my ass a little bit more, as if he was marking his territory. As a man, I should be fighting against that, but I wasn't. I wasn't a man anymore.

He stood up slowly and then, alongside Gears, they jerked off until they were coming all over me. I felt their come hitting every part of me, coating me in white with it, and I came again. I had another climax, and it was like my body was never going to recover from it.

It was convulsing and shaking, and it was also so sweaty that my hands were slipping on the floor.

When they were done, they were still smiling devilishly.

Noticing that this was almost ending, I decided to propose something, even though I had no idea if they were going to accept it or not. If I was going to become their bitch, then I needed to make it so I could have my voice heard sometimes.

"Daddies, can I suck you off until you are clean?" I asked and my heart was already tight. It was always so difficult when I had no idea what their answer was going to be. Even though I could bring them more pleasure than they ever felt before, they could say no just to torment me a little more.

They looked at each other and then responded, "Sure thing, but be quick about it. We don't want to waste time, especially because we have another prize in sight."

I proceeded to do what I'd proposed, sucking and licking them until they were clean, all the while thinking that when they said that, they were talking about my wife. It couldn't be anyone else,

and I wasn't even sad or angry about it. It was just right.
Everything was happening as it should be.

CHAPTER 6

I was outside, by the swimming pool. Why was I here? The answer was obvious and it was right at the tip of my tongue. They wanted me outside, naked, and with the buttplug still in my ass because they wanted everyone to know that they owned me. We had some neighbors and they were nice, friendly people. When they looked out their windows and saw me for who I was now, they would notice that something was wrong with me.

And instead of calling the police or rushing over to try and help me, when they saw the massive bikers pounding in and out of my ass, they would find themselves stuck where they were, incapable of moving. Even though I didn't ask the bikers if that was their plan, I was pretty sure that it was part of it at least.

It was for that reason that my body was already shaking when I heard the bikers stepping toward me. They came out the back of the house, closing the kitchen door behind them. They were naked and my wife was in tow. She was right behind them and as naked as they were. It was almost like they were in a competition to find out who could look more naked, even though that was impossible. They already had no clothes on.

"I know how impatient you're getting, waiting for so long," Forger said and, in his hand, he was holding what appeared to be a bottle of lube. I shouldn't even know what it was, especially because I never fucked my wife in her ass.

And thinking about her again, she plopped down on a reclining chair by the swimming pool, with a pair of sunglasses on and then I noticed that she was also bringing with her a coconut, from which she took controlled sips.

She was definitely enjoying this, much more than she should be.

"I've been waiting for you, Masters," I confessed and someone that knew me before this would be saying that something was deeply wrong with me, even though nothing was. I just found my calling and that was all it was.

"It's like I promised you before. We are going to fuck you so hard that you won't be able to walk for days," Forger threatened, but his threat didn't concern me. Actually, it only turned me on even more than I already was. My prick was stiff and leaking pre-cum. They didn't have any reason to look down at it and find it, but they still did.

"And we should probably do something about that as well," Gears said and when I wondered if he was going to add to that or not, he decided to answer my question, "by putting a chastity cage on you. I'm already deciding on the right model for you."

A chastity cage locking my junk inside of it? I didn't know what was about it, but the mere thought of that happening was already hitting all the right buttons in me. And thinking that, I couldn't contain it any longer. I started to come, my cock convulsing and smearing the floor around the swimming pool. I should be feeling ashamed of that, but just like with everything that was happening here, I wasn't. I wasn't going to be when it was my calling.

"You are always so funny you make me question why we didn't find it before," Gears said, walking until he was behind me.

I was on all fours, and I felt him squatting behind me. I felt his hands gripping my ass, just like it happened that time when he eased the buttplug into my orifice. Now that I was thinking about it, when was that?

It was difficult to keep track of the passage of time, especially when I was living the best moment of my life under the scrutiny of these bikers. And if there was something even more rewarding than that? It was the fact that I would do it all over again.

"Yes, Master. I'm funny for you and you only."

He chuckled behind me, his fingers moving around my waist, feeling my backside, and then looking for my orifice. He played with it for a little while, but it wasn't enough.

I felt my back arching again and then my prick was unloading my cream one more time, but even that wasn't enough as well. I needed more. I needed him inside of me, and I knew he was going to do that.

"Damn, if you are always so willing and easy, then you are probably even better than Sandra," he chuckled and even though it was a joke, Sandra shot her hand over her head, taking off her sunglasses right away.

"Hey, I heard that. I don't try to compete against my puny little husband, but if you want to, then I can join in on the fun."

Gears craned his head slightly to look at her, his finger going inside my orifice and then poking me in there, rubbing against my walls.

"Don't worry about it, princess. You still have something that he doesn't, and that's more than enough to keep you at the top."

I knew what he was talking about, and it was a topic of pain for me. He was talking about having a pussy, which was something I wanted to have. Maybe, one day, science would be advanced enough so that I could implant it, and I'd pay any price to make that happen, but it wasn't a reality at the moment.

She shook her head and then Gears eased the buttplug out of my ass. I almost didn't see that happening, and when I did, it was almost too late. I felt like something was missing, and I knew that it was the item that he was now holding in his calloused hand.

"It's clean, just like I thought it was," he pointed out and it was something that made me feel proud of it.

In the meantime, Forger walked until he was standing in front of me and then he grabbed his prick, stroking it. He was giving it slow, controlled strokes, and he was enticing me to suck him off, something I wanted to do right at this moment.

"You are thinking about this, aren't you?" He asked and I nodded. There was no point in wasting any time, so I just wrapped my lips around his mushroom-shaped cockhead, closing my eyes for I knew I was falling into a world of complete, rewarding bliss.

In the meantime, his friend was already gripping my waist and then tugging me to him slightly, nudging my waiting orifice with his oversized dick. In a moment, he was already inside of me and I knew that I just lost my last virginity. I knew he was going to be ramming in and out of me so hard I would never be the same, and that was okay.

"Holy shit, you are still so tight. I knew that using the buttplug was necessary, but it's like it made no difference, even though, had I not used it, you would be even tighter than you are now," he mumbled more to himself than to me and then started to pound in and out of me, his pace frenetic and too fast from the get-go.

Meanwhile, his body was destroying my mouth and that was putting it mildly. He was turning my mouth into his plaything and was so focused on it so much that I wasn't surprised when he was coming inside of it, giving me the salty taste I was looking for. I savored all of it and it couldn't have been any different.

In the meantime, while his body was ravaging my ass and slapping his balls against my butt cheeks, he didn't hold back when he started to cream inside of me.

His hot, scorching ropes of come filled me to the brim, and I wouldn't have it any differently. Each rope of come that helped him with his goal brought me closer to my orgasm, and I also didn't hold back when I started to come one more time, which was something that never happened before in my life. It was like I was years younger than I was now.

When I was done, I was panting. In the meantime, Gears jammed his prick inside of me one last, destructive time, hitting my prostate. He wasn't even careful about that and it hurt, more so than I thought it was going to.

And yet, it was going to leave a good, lasting mark on me.

EPILOGUE

"**W**hat the hell is the meaning of this?" My best friend asked, thinking that something like this shouldn't be happening. It should never be happening. He always thought that I was the manliest, strongest man he knew, and now he was seeing me like this, in this humiliating and yet rewarding position. I was on my knees in front of the couch, and my former wife was sitting on it. She had her legs on me and was eating popcorn from a huge bowl.

Now that I was nothing more than the submissive little prick I was, she could do anything she wanted with me. She was watching something on the TV, and it was probably a romance movie. She was enjoying it and barely paying attention to Gerald.

He had just opened the door and stepped into the house, glancing at me and then at her. She was naked from top to bottom, and I could tell that it was having quite the effect on him, especially because his bulge was showing. It was something he tried to keep hidden whenever he could, but it wasn't working at the moment.

Glancing down at it, I could see how massive he was, though it was nowhere near the size of the bikers'. It wasn't that I thought it was anything close to their size, but I still found it a little disappointing.

And yet, it was big enough to make me feel hard. I was hoping he could join us here, but given the look of surprise on his face, I didn't think he was going to. After all, he was engaged to his fiancée and I doubted he was going to change his mind about the marriage, which was as disappointing as finding out that he wasn't as big as the bikers.

"I just found out I'm gay. Sandra isn't my wife anymore," I confessed and he blinked twice. It was obvious that he didn't understand what I just said, but it was okay.

Soon, he was going to make sense of all this and when he did, when he found out how good gay sex was, then he would come back. In the meantime, I could only salivate at the thought of that happening.

"What?" He asked, sounding just as dumbfounded as before.

"He said that he's ours," a rumbling voice echoed in the living room, coming from the kitchen. That was Gears, who was also holding a bowl of popcorn in his right hand. He threw a popcorn kernel toward me and his aim was so good that it went right into my mouth, and I chewed it down like the good little pet I was.

When it came down to it, this was always supposed to be happening.

Gerald glanced at Gears, his eyes going up and down. It was obvious that the last thing he thought he was going to see in my house was such a massive, imposing tattooed man stepping into the living room. He was also naked and hard. I knew he was going to be fucking my wife in front of me and I was waiting for it. Before this, it was incredibly humiliating, but now... not anymore.

"And who the hell are you?" He asked, his cheeks flushing. He couldn't stop staring at the biker's crotch, and it showed me that he also knew he was bigger.

The biker was so much bigger that he put his much smaller cock to shame, and that was impressive in and of itself. I wanted it back inside my mouth, but I had no idea if today he was going to be so merciful with me.

He plopped down onto the couch and then also threw his legs over my backside. I was supporting the weight of his legs and also my wife's, and I was doing a good job at it. If there was something I always wanted to do with my life, it was serving them.

"I'm her new husband," he replied, pecking her cheek right in front of Gerald, and also of me. There was something about it that made my dick stir and shake, and I could imagine myself jerking it until I came.

The only problem with that was that I didn't think they were going to allow me to do that. After all, the chastity cage was sturdy and it couldn't be moved or changed. Not without the key, which he had in his pocket.

"This doesn't make any sense," Gerald said, turning around and when he was going to walk out of the house, an imposing figure appeared in front of him. It turned out that it was none other than Forger, who was also naked even though he was outside this whole time. The neighbors were afraid of him, so they never called the police on him. Even though he would go to jail if that happened, they knew that he would be released soon, and thus they preferred not to take the risk.

"Going anywhere, little buddy?" He asked and Gerald's eyes snapped down, finding his gargantuan and impressive rod pointing at him.

It was mean and raging, and even though he was straight, he couldn't help but wonder just what... it would feel like... if he put it in his mouth, even if only for a little, quick taste.

"No, I think not," and then he stepped back into the house, looking concerned and flabbergasted, but also definitely enjoying the direction this was taking.

I was finally going to be able to suck him off, too!

The End

Looking for more stories like this one? Then, check these out.

1. Caught Looking by the Quarterback

2. Caught Looking by the Basketeer

3. Caught Looking by the Dropout

4. Caught Looking by the Jock

5. Caught Looking by the Roommate

You can also find a sneak peek for book 1 on the next page. Lastly, leave a review if you liked the book. Your feedback helps me improve!

SNEAK PEEK: CAUGHT LOOKING BY THE QUARTERBACK

Straight to Gay First Time Story (Bicurious Guys - 1)

I was just a college guy, like all the others. I was trying to fit in and look less like an idiot. Why did I have to stumble into the college's football team, though? I didn't know, but things were working out this way. More and more girls were beginning to show interest in me, even if it was only momentary... and I didn't think it was going to lead anywhere.

I sighed, closing the door by my side when I realized someone was there. Not too far from me, taking off his shirt and getting ready to put on his uniform. I supposed it was appreciation more than anything that was making me feel this way about the guy, even though I was 100% straight. Really, I was, and nothing was going to change that.

But nothing could have gotten me ready for what I was seeing. The guy was perfect. He was in his early twenties, so he was a little older than me, huge, with rippling muscles, and a beard still to be made. His hair was jet-black and his eyes the color of emerald. Every time he looked at me, he froze me with his gaze.

I couldn't stop thinking about him, even when he was in his room and wasn't doing anything more than playing on his computer. I wasn't going to say I was gay. I really wasn't, but I couldn't stop admiring him for being everything I wanted to become. Perhaps he could help me with working out at the gym, but then I didn't know if I'd be able to hide my boner... like it was happening now.

Not only I wasn't gay, but I also had to keep reminding myself that I wasn't a virgin, either. Not in the usual, more common sense of the word, at least. I had some experiences where it kind of happened with some girls... And I'd like to keep things at that.

Austin was now taking off his pants too, and I couldn't stop dissecting his perfect legs with my eyes. I couldn't help but imagine what it would be like to slide my hands over his muscles, feeling his hair, the curves that defined his legs, and smelling the scent of his crotch. Why was I thinking about those things of my team's leader?

I didn't know, but I was already feeling desperate and my boner was beginning to show. I came here with a common pair of jeans and it should be enough to keep it hidden. Austin could never find out that I had a huge turn-on for him, or else there would be trouble. This was a small college in the middle of nowhere, in a region known for being pretty homophobic. I didn't want to take the risk and then be forced to transfer to another university. It wasn't going to happen.

I took a deep breath and looked away quickly when he turned slightly. I didn't know if he was looking at me or not. We were in the dresser room and everything was pretty quiet here. Everything was so silent I could almost hear a pin dropping. I was a couple of feet away from Austin and I was pretty sure he wasn't thinking anything odd was happening here. After all, he had no reason to believe I was gay.

I took a deep breath in, looked back where he was, and I

realized he was back to putting on his uniform. But he was still taking off his socks this time. He wasn't looking as imperious as before because he was seated now, his back turned to me.

But it wasn't that seeing him that way was making him look any less lust-inducing than he was. Even now, my body was frozen and I hadn't made much progress in terms of putting on my uniform. I needed to do that when my cock wasn't so hard. I should be punching myself that I was feeling those things for the guy that was always so willing to help everyone out, but it was just… impossible to control my feelings.

I heard the door opening and I knew that meant that things here were going to get more complicated. I could hear them talking out loud, cracking jokes, and laughing. It was the rest of the team. They were walking into the dressing room and were going to see that I was stealing glances at the quarterback…

BICURIOUS SERIES AND MORE

GAY FOR BLUE COLLARS

1. Given to the Cop

2. Given to the Miner

3. Given to the Plumber

4. Given to the Firefighter

5. Given to the Mechanic

DIRTY FANTASIES

1. Filling in for the Bride

2. Filling in for the Wife

3. Filling in for the Girlfriend

ABOUT THE AUTHOR

Steamy MM stories, baby! Michael Levi can't go a day without sitting down and putting into words all the dirty scenes that sprout in his mind. His collection is diverse, but it's gay love only. And if you are looking for something free, check his mailing list. Warning: it can be extra spicy.

When Michael Levi isn't writing, he's chilling out by the lake close to his house. Nothing better than kicking back with a martini in his hand as he daydreams his next explicit scenes.